For all who look up, and wonder
—M. L. R.

And for Linda Zuckerman,
who showed me where to look
—M. F.

BEACH LANE BOOKS
An imprint of Simon & Schuster Children's Publishing Division
1230 Avenue of the Americas, New York, New York 10020
Text copyright © 2011 by Mary Lyn Ray
Illustrations copyright © 2011 by Marla Frazee
All rights reserved, including the right of reproduction in whole or in
part in any form.
BEACH LANE BOOKS is a trademark of Simon & Schuster, Inc.
For information about special discounts for bulk purchases, please
contact Simon & Schuster Special Sales at 1-866-506-1949 or
business@simonandschuster.com.
The Simon & Schuster Speakers Bureau can bring authors to your live
event. For more information or to book an event, contact the Simon &
Schuster Speakers Bureau at 1-866-248-3049 or visit our website at
www.simonspeakers.com.
Book design by Marla Frazee and Ann Bobco
The text for this book was hand-lettered by Marla Frazee.
The illustrations for this book are rendered in graphite, gouache,
and gel pens on Strathmore 2-ply hot press paper.
Manufactured in USA
0318 PCR

11
Library of Congress Cataloging-in-Publication Data
Ray, Mary Lyn.
Stars / Mary Lyn Ray ; illustrated by Marla Frazee. — 1st ed.
p. cm.
Summary: Explores the wonder of stars, whether they are in the night
sky, on a plant as a promise of fruit to come, or in one's pocket for
those days when one does not feel shiny.
ISBN 978-1-4424-2249-0 (hardcover)
ISBN 978-1-4424-3578-0 (eBook)
[1. Stars—Fiction.] I. Frazee, Marla, ill. II. Title.
PZ7.R210154St 2011
[E]—dc22
2010033253

STARS

BY MARY LYN RAY AND MARLA FRAZEE

BEACH LANE BOOKS

NEW YORK LONDON TORONTO SYDNEY

A star is how you know it's almost night.

As soon as you see one, there's another, and another.

And the dark
that comes
doesn't feel so
dark.

What if you could have a star?
They shine like little silver eggs
you could gather in a basket.

Except you know you can't. Not really.

But you can draw a star on
shiny paper and cut around it.
Then you can put it in your pocket.

Having a star
in your pocket
is like having
your best rock
in your pocket,
but
different.

Because
a star
is different
from a
rock.

Pin a star on your shirt
and you can be sheriff.

Put a star on a stick
and you've made a wand.

If you hold a wand the right way,
you might see a wish come true.

Not always.
Only sometimes.

You never know
about a
wish.

You can give a star to a friend.

But never give away
the one you keep in your pocket.

You need to know it is there.

Some days you feel shiny as a star.
If you've done something important,
people may call you a star.

But some days
you don't feel
shiny.

Those days,
it's good
to reach
for the one
in your
pocket.

If you ever lose your star,
you can draw another.
Or you can find one.

There are places.

Moss where you might see fairies
is made of green stars.

White stars in June grass

Yellow stars on pumpkin vines

become strawberries in July.

become October pumpkins.

Snowflakes
are
stars.

Blow a ball of dandelion and you blow
a thousand stars into the sky.

A button
can have a
star on it.

And if you always
brush your teeth,
someone might give you
a red or green or blue
or gold or silver star.

There might be a
star on the calendar
to mark a special day.

But stars that
    come with night —
        for those
            you have
            to wait
            for night.

                    You need
                    some dark
                    to see
                    them.

It may help to
have on pajamas.

Then you look up. Almost always you will find one.

And another   and another.
                  and another

And if sometimes you can't see them,

they're still there.

Every night.

Everywhere.